Grade School Super Hero

The Complete Trilogy

Justin Johnson

Grade School Super Hero: The Complete Trilogy

Justin Johnson

I greatly appreciate you taking the time to read my work. Please consider leaving a review wherever you bought the book, or telling your friends or blog readers about this book, to help me spread the word.

Thank you for supporting my work.

Justin Johnson

GET YOUR FREE BOOK!

For your free copy of the #1 Best Seller Farty Marty,
go to www.justinjohnsonauthor.com

TABLE OF CONTENTS

A SHORT STORY FOR KIDS AGES 9-12

GRADE SCHOOL
SUPER HERO

JUSTIN JOHNSON

GRADE SCHOOL SUPER HERO

Have you ever wished you were a super hero?

Let me guess, you want to fly, right?

Or, perhaps, you wish you could take a lickin' and keep on tickin'?

No?

You say it's the ability run as fast as you can and get all the awards for saving the day.

Well I'm here to tell you that it's not all it's cracked up to be. Infact, sometimes I think my gift, as they call it, is the worst thing that ever happened to me.

I mean, there I was, little Johnny Williams — JW, as they call me — waiting on third base for my best friend Sheila to kick me home. We were playing the end of the day kickball game.

Any kid that looked over toward our teacher, Mrs. Delfin, knew that this was going to be it. If Sheila didn't kick this ball into the outfield, that whistle in Mrs. Delfin's mouth was going to blow and the game would end in a tie. I don't know how many end of the day kickball games you've ever been a part of, but I can tell you that a tie is worse than losing.

At least when you lose, you know you've lost. Not to mention, half the kids feel good about winning. But when you tie, everybody walks head down back into the building to get their things to go home, wondering what could've been.

I had my foot on the bag, one eye on Sheila and the other on Mrs. Delfin. Sheila kicked the ball and it dribbled forward toward the pitcher, Donald. Certainly not her best effort.

I took off toward home plate and saw Donald looking at the catcher, Billy. I rolled my eyes thinking that he wasn't really very good at this. For one, he had a sure out if he threw the ball to first. For another, I didn't have to run as there was no one else on base.

My right eye caught the glimpse of Mrs. Delfin's whistle bobbing up and down between her teeth. This was it. I had to leave the safety of the third base and make a run for it.

Donald threw the ball toward Billy, who shrugged a 'What are you doing?' in Donald's direction and then threw the ball down the first base line where Sheila was already safe.

Roger, the first baseman, threw the ball back to Billy. I was already half way down the baseline, wondering what in the world I'd done. I had a tough choice to make. Sure, we could have had Greg come up and kick me in, but the way that whistle was bobbing back and forth, I knew we didn't have much time left — and Greg wasn't going to get his turn anyway.

And then we go back to the tie thing. Even if it couldn't be my team, it could be someone's team that won.   Someone should feel good at the end of the day, right?

Well, the ball came in and the catcher and the third base men took turns throwing the ball at me and missing. And then the catcher got smart. He stood in front of home plate, holding the ball, waiting for me to either get back on base or challenge him.

I saw Mrs. Delfin pull in a large breath of air. She was going to blow the whistle. This was it.

I took off running and then it happened.

As I got closer to home, I knew that I was going to have to do something incredible. When I was about three feet away from Billy, I jumped, not really sure what that was going to do. I'd never had any amazing physical abilities.

But on this day, I flew.

Well, not really flew. But I jumped right over Billy and landed perfectly safe on home plate. Both feet hit the middle of the base as Mrs. Delfin sent air through the whistle, making us the winners!

You may have already guessed it, but this was the moment I realized I was a super hero.

* * *

Of course, it couldn't have been a private revelation.

Everybody saw it...EVERYBODY!

The teachers who were lining their classes up saw it. The kids who were lining up to go inside saw it. The kids playing kickball definitely saw it. Even the kids who were serving detention inside saw it and were gathered at the windows of the school.

And within a few days, even the kids who hadn't seen it had found out from one friend or another.

You might think that it's pretty cool to be able to do something that other people can't. And I don't want to discourage you, it definitely has its good points. But I do think you should be aware of some of the drawbacks.

Walking down the hall for normal kids is just walking down the hall. But walking down the hall for me became a struggle. With so many kids wanting to talk to me about my new found talent, it was like swimming against the current every time I had to go to the bathroom or get to class.

By the time third period rolled around, I was exhausted.

And then everybody wanted to see me jump. They'd follow it up with, "You know...like you did on the playground?"

They didn't really need to say this. Somehow, I had already guessed what they were talking about.

I'd have to disappoint them and tell them that I needed to get to class. The collective groans of disappointment really started to grate on me. I was a people pleaser by nature.

So one day, I told everybody that I would do it — one time only — on the playground at the end of the day.

The crowd gathered around. Not a kid could be seen swinging or sliding or playing tag. All eyes were on me. Even the teachers.

I don't know if the adrenaline rush that comes with being on display in front of a large group of people had anything to do with what happened next, but I thought it might've had something to do with it.

I prepared to make my jump, figuring I'd just jump over the kids who'd formed the circle and land on the other side of them.

I bent my knees and clenched my fists. I swallowed hard and let my legs spring back.

I could hear the oohs and aahs as I took off.

They may have had that reaction anyway. But their reaction had very little to do with the fact that I'd simply jumped over them. It had more to do with the fact that I had, more or less, flown to the top of the school.

I stood there in shock.

For one, I am deathly afraid of heights. I prefer to be on the ground whenever possible. It just seems like there's far less chance of injury that way.

Once I'd semi-adjusted to my circumstances, I took a deep breath and a look around. I could see the whole city from where I was standing. I was looking at the tops of buildings and a smoggy horizon in ways I had never thought possible.

The thought occurred to me to test things out and jump from the roof and see how far I could fly before I fell. And then the fear of heights and the idea of what that fall might do to me entered into the equation.

I looked over the side of the building at my teachers and classmates. It was kind of funny.   The kids were all waving me down, encouraging me to "just jump already!" My teachers on the other hand were putting their hands up, telling me to, "stop and stay there until we can get somebody to come up and get you!"

It was easy to listen to the teachers and just wait for someone to come get me.

In the end, Mr. Lipscolm, the principal of the school, came and opened the access door. I walked through with him, relieved that everyone had seen me do this. Somehow I thought I was finished using this newly found set of skills.

I was wrong.

* * *

That night, when my homework was finished, I joined my parents at the table for dinner. The food was on the stove and plates were on the counter next to it. My parents had already piled their plate high with mashed potatoes and chuck roast.

They were absentmindedly shoveling in heaps of potatoes as they stared at the TV that was mounted to the wall next to the table.

I was scooping the roast onto my plate when I heard their forks fall from their hands and clang on their plates.

"What's wrong?" I asked, as I turned to see what was bothering them.

Neither of them answered, but the man on the TV was explaining everything.

His story was a little long, and honestly, I can't remember everything that he said. But I'll give you the important details.

Basically, there was an asteroid the size of Europe headed for Earth. It was threatening to wipe out 20% of the population on impact and the rest would fall away in the weeks and months following as a result of the environmental damage it would do. Humans were going to be the new dinosaurs.

As if that wasn't bad enough, the central location for the initial impact was my school.

* * *

It was a hard night of sleep. I tossed and turned, dreading the trip to school the next day. I was thinking that I was the only one who would possibly be able to stop this asteroid from destroying everyone.

Let me tell you, not even Santa Claus on Christmas eve will give you a tougher night of sleep than this thought.

And then it occurred to me that I wasn't even really sure what all of my powers were — or if I even had any other powers besides being able to jump really high. Had I even really flown earlier, or was that just a super jump.

I didn't know.

Uncertainty kept me awake.

I stared at the wall in the dark. The President had been on the television telling the American citizens that nothing could be done and we should all do our best to hunker down and be with our families until the asteroid hit. He gave us less than two days.

I made up my mind. I was going to stop that thing, or, at the very least, give it the best try I could. It didn't make any sense to just sit by and be part of something horrible if there was a way I might be able to help.

I may have been unsure of my powers. But being sure of certain death made it worth the risk.

* * *

When I got to school the next day, the principal, Mr. Lipscolm, was standing at the top of the front steps of the school. He was looking at me, and I knew exactly what he wanted.

I gave him a thumbs up and said, "I'm on it."

He nodded as I walked by.

Sheila caught up to me as I was putting my backpack in my locker.

"Did you hear the news?" she asked.

I nodded.

"I'm so scared," she said. "I don't even feel like I should be here, but my parents made me come. They said it would be good to keep things as normal as possible. Honestly, I think they're in denial about the whole thing."

I nodded again, not wanting to look at her. She was my best friend. I'd known her since we were four and we played with the Play-Doh together on the first day of preschool.

The weight of what I was about to do was really starting to set in. I was dreading it.

And I was afraid.

I finally forced myself to look at Sheila and I saw that she was crying. I began crying too.

"I'm going to try to stop it," I said.

"You can't! There's no way...you'll die," she argued.

I wiped my eyes with the sleeve of my shirt and said, "If I don't do anything, we'll all share the same fate anyway. At least this way I'm giving people a chance."

"No," she said. "I won't let you."

"I'm afraid you're going to have just let me go on this one."

I could see her thinking. After years of friendship, I was pretty good at telling when Sheila's gears were turning.

"Okay," she finally said. She gave me a hug and kissed my cheek. "Before you go..."

Before she could finish her thought, her eyes welled with tears again and she broke down sobbing.

"I know," I said, putting my hand on her shoulder.

With that, I left my best friend in the middle of the hallway and headed toward the playground doors.

* * *

It was a warm day. The smog was heavy in the air, making it difficult to see anything in the sky.

I had to test my flying ability first.

Jumping up about four feet off the ground, I hovered. I spun around in place, never touching the ground.

I wondered if I could go higher from this spot, so I raised my hands up into the air. Much to my surprise, I began to rise. A little at first, and then quite fast.

I put my arms down and pointed them at the ground and began to go down.

I'd like to say my landing was smooth, but it wasn't. Standing up, I wiped the grass from my pants and shirt and headed for the playground equipment.

I wanted to test my strength. I figured, it would be enough to just fly up to the asteroid and blow on it. I would probably have to be strong enough to move it.

There was a slide facing the back corner of the playground. It was one of those twisty slides that always makes your hair stand up on end. I reached for the bottom of the slide and gave it a pull upwards.

To my surprise, the whole playset lifted up with it. Even more to my surprise, was that it didn't even feel heavy. It felt like I was lifting a pillow.

It was time.

I put the playset down and headed for the center of the field. Raising my hands up toward the sky, I took off and made my way though the smog and clouds.

I looked down briefly, to get one final look at the school. And then I put my head up and set my sights on that stupid asteroid.

* * *

What's your take on hot things? I guess, I would have to say I'm kind of a wimp with hot. I like warm. I even like really warm. But when something's hot, it really bothers me.

My mother and father have always joked about my sensitive little hands.

Let me tell you, that asteroid was hot, hot, hot. I had located it and was now in the process of pushing it back into space. That's great and all, and I'm pretty sure my body was now fire proof as a result of my newly found powers.

Unfortunately, that didn't mean that I wasn't able feel the heat.

And as I pushed this massive hot rock away from everyone, there was stuff flying off it in my direction. Little crumbs of heat hitting me in the legs and forehead.

At one point, I had to close my eyes, just to make sure that I didn't get an ember in the eye. It was horrible.

The only thought that got me through everything was that I was saving humanity. Which, I suppose, would be enough to get anyone through a task like this.

The farther I went with the asteroid, the weirder I began to feel. My hands and face continued to be battered and beaten with the lava like heat, while my legs and feet were begin to freeze like popsicles from the coldness of space.

I felt like an icy hot pack.

I was starting to wonder how much longer I would have to do this, when I decided to let go and see what would happen.

To my relief, the asteroid was now far enough out and the lack of gravity in space had allowed it to have its direction changed. I watched as it floated harmlessly out into space and away from Earth.

Thank goodness, I said to myself.

And then my whole body started to freeze.

I put my arms down toward the Earth and began my flight home.

* * *

Let me tell you about re-entry. Have you ever come inside in the wintertime? Say you built a snowman, or went sledding, or played some football in the snow. You know how your nose starts snotting everywhere and you can't control it? And then mom puts a mug of soup or hot cocoa in front of you and opens up the flood gates.

Yeah, that was me....times a million!

And the burning and tingling that went through my whole body was horrible. It was like fiery pins and needles.

Everyone was waiting for me out on the playground when I came down. They all looked like they were preparing to hug me. And they came running at me when I landed. But upon sight of the massive amounts of snot running down my face, they stopped and gave me friendly waves and thanks from a distance.

Honestly, my nose was running like Niagara Falls.

Sheila, however, did brave the elements and hug me. As I was hugging her, I noticed that my hands were still smoking and full of blisters. But considering I'd just pushed an asteroid that was a million degrees, I thought it could've been worse.

It was pretty cool to be treated like a hero. Everybody was saying great job and there were pats on the back all around and things like that.

They threw a special parade in my honor and gave me a key to the city.

I even got to meet the President of the United States!

And all that's pretty cool.

But if you were to ask me if it was worth it...I'd have to say no.

Being a super hero just isn't all it's cracked up to be.

A SHORT STORY FOR KIDS AGES 9-12
GRADE SCHOOL
SUPER HERO 2
HERE WE GO AGAIN
JUSTIN JOHNSON

GRADE SCHOOL SUPER HERO 2
HERE WE GO AGAIN

Hey there.

It's JW here again.

I have to be honest with you. Not a lot has happened in my life since my last adventure. For those of you who may not have heard about it, or those of you who don't remember, here's a quick recap:

Basically, I found out I had super powers on the playground one day when I jumped over a kid playing kickball. After that, everyone wanted to see how super my powers were, so I did a quick demonstration. As a result of this demonstration, I ended up jumping so high that I wound up on top of the school and the principal had to come and rescue me.

Then, as fate would have it, I watched the news with my parents one night and discovered that there was a massive asteroid heading for Earth...and the results of such a thing were going to be catastrophic. So I decided to take care of it...which I did. And everyone was crazy happy and they put on parades and celebrations and I even got to meet the President of the United States of America.

There's just one problem: I didn't really enjoy any of it.

So, now you're caught up and we can get on with the next adventure in my super hero existence.

You know, there's a funny thing about fame. It's short lived. People forget all about you unless you're in the news doing something amazing (or not amazing). The same things happened with me.

About three weeks after I saved the world from utter destruction and annihilation, people stopped asking me about it. They stopped asking me to jump to the top of the school again and they stopped asking me to pick up the playground equipment. Even the questions about the White House and how it was to see the President of the United States stopped.

I was just plain old JW again.

And, honestly, I was pretty happy about that.

It was great. I was left alone when I walked down the hallways at school and I could make it to class on time. Sheila and I were able to hang out like we used to and it was great.

This amazing feeling of calm and normalcy that had found its way back into my life would be, unfortunately, short lived.

* * *

I remember it clearly. Probably more clearly than I would have normally, but I was studying in my room for my mid year exams at school. And let me tell you, super hero or not, I'm really bad at math and I needed all the help I could get.

Hunkered down on my bed, books splayed open, pencil in hand, I was immersed in numbers and equations I didn't fully — or even partially — understand. My eyes were starting to glaze over and everything was becoming a blur, so I decided to take a five minute break and head downstairs for a piece of toast with ketchup. At this point, I would really appreciate it if you could see past your own issues with ketchup on your toast and just understand that I really like it. Thank you.

My parents as usual were sitting in the kitchen. Dinner was over and the dishes were washed. They were sitting at the table, watching the evening news on TV. Dad was doubling down on the news and reading the newspaper, while mom was working on knitting a pair of little booties for some lady she worked with who had just had a baby.

The woman on the news was talking about a tropical storm of sorts and how it was mere days away from hitting the coast of the city where I lived.

This felt like Deja Vu all over again.

I could feel the world closing in around me. My head felt light, like a floating balloon and I was getting dizzy.

Unsure if this was a result of too much studying, or the possible impact of the news story I'd just seen, I decided it was time to go to bed.

I kissed my mom and dad goodnight and headed upstairs to brush my teeth before putting on my pajamas and heading to bed.

Laying there on my pillow, it became quite clear that it was not the test that had me shaken.

Visions of people fleeing a giant storm and the devastation it would leave in its wake were dominating my thoughts. Imagining the destruction it would have on everyone, my mind opened up and allowed me to see a boy. This boy was my age, standing in the middle of the street. He was hurt, walking with a limp and looking around for his family. There was panic in his eyes that I would not be able to forget anytime soon.

* * *

I don't remember falling asleep, but when I woke up it felt like I did nothing but toss and turn all night. My hair was disheveled, standing up in the oddest places, my sheets were all over the floor as if they'd just been tossed about by a giant, and I had a sharp pain where the base of my neck met my shoulders.

It had been a rough night alright.

And as if that wasn't bad enough, when I looked at the clock, it read 8:35, which left me less than ten minutes to get to school.

This day was going to be a doozy.

I managed to get out the door in a matter of minutes, but I was not looking good. I was what one might call a train wreck. My left shoe was untied, the socks on my feet didn't match and I put so much water in my hair in an effort to calm it down, that I now had droplets of water dripping all over my face and down the back of my shirt.

Sheila looked at me when I arrived at homeroom a few minutes late. To be fair to Sheila, everyone looked at me when I came through the door. My grand entrance was a sight to behold.

"What in the world happened to you?"

"Don't ask," I responded curtly. "Just know that it's probably closer to what you're thinking than you know."

She nodded and went back to her book. I noticed it was our math book.

"Oh shoot!" I shouted out, considerably louder than I had wanted to. Noticing that nearly everyone — alright, it was everyone — looked up from what they were doing to take notice, I brought my voice back down to a whisper. "I totally forgot all about that last night."

"You mean, you didn't study? JW, you're terrible at math. How are you going to pass the test without studying?"

I knew Sheila was right, but I just couldn't stop thinking about that storm and those families and that boy in the middle of everything all by himself. It all kind of made the test seem pretty trivial.

"There's something I have to tell you about," I told Sheila.

She put her finger up in the air, prompting me to wait a minute while she finished reading a section from her math notes.

"Is it important, or can it wait?" she finally asked.

I had to admit to myself that there was really no way I was going to be able to do anything about this coming storm now. The news woman had said that it was still a few days away.

"It can wait," I said.

She didn't seem too interested in anything other than cramming for the test anyway, and from the looks of homeroom this morning, everyone else had only math on their minds as well.

I took out my notebook and began to study.

* * *

"That test wasn't so hard," Sheila bragged as we headed down the steps toward freedom.

I was silent.

I was not in agreement with my friend Sheila, for the first time in a long time.

"How do you think you did, JW?"

"Let's not talk about it," I said, embarrassed.

We walked for a few minutes in silence past the tall buildings that were as tall as the sky. I was looking up toward the top of one such building that seemed to be touching the clouds.   I was wondering what would happen to it if the storm was as big as the news woman said.

Would anything happen?

Would it be flooded by water from the ocean?

Would it be knocked over by the high winds and debris?

"Whatcha thinking'?" Sheila said, thankfully interrupting my thoughts.

"I was thinking about that building falling over," I said pointing upward.

"Why?" she said, a look of confusion stretching across her face.

"I saw something on the news last night that has me a little shaken," I admitted.

"What's that?"

"There's a storm coming. It's a few days off now, but it's fixing to mess up the coast of the city pretty good." Sheila walked in silence, just listening to me ramble. "I can't shake these visions from my mind. I keep seeing these buildings being destroyed, our city in ruins and kids just like us left with nothing."

"So, what're you thinking? That you have to do something?"

"That's exactly what I'm thinking," I said. "It worked last time. I mean, if I can handle an asteroid, I should be able to handle a storm, right?"

I ventured a glance at her and noticed that she was wearing her doubt face.

"What?" I said, "You don't think I can do it?"

"It's not that I don't think you can do it, it's that I have no idea how you would do it?"

"Did you have any idea how I was going to handle the asteroid?"

"No, not really...but somehow, it seemed more doable than taking on a widespread storm. I mean, with the asteroid, as long as you were able to get up to it and touch it without burning your face off, you could move it. Because it was essentially a giant rock. But this..."

"I'm listening."

"This," she continued, "is going to be harder to harness. You have nothing to put your focus on. The wind? How do you stop the wind? Or the rain? Or anything else that might come along with it?"

"I don't know," I admitted. "But from the sounds of things, I have two days to figure it out."

* * *

The next two days went by so fast. It's funny how things work in the kid world, or any world for that matter. When you're looking forward to doing something, two days can drag on forever. But when you're not looking forward to doing something, as I wasn't with the whole storm thing, those days seem to go by in the blink of an eye.

The worst part about everything was that I had not a clue about how I was going to take on the storm. I thought and thought and wracked my brain over things for the past two days and still...nothing.

At this point, I was running up against a very powerful emotion. One that had led to both successes and failures of epic proportions...hope.

I was hoping that this storm might just change its course last minute and float back to sea harmlessly, without so much as a single raindrop hitting the pavement. I was hoping that someone would be able to step up and take care of the situation at hand, leaving me free to go to school and do the normal kid stuff I'd rather be doing.

And then there was the last hope. The one I was really banking on to help me through this: I was hoping that somehow I had powers I'd not yet discovered.

I didn't really have any idea what those powers might be, but I was hoping that I could conjure something from deep within that would help take care of this impossible task.

Sheila was at the top of the stairs looking down at me. I felt haggard and worn as I trudged step by step up to the doors.

"You look like you've already been hit by the storm," she joked. I could tell it was something she didn't want to joke about. She had spent the better part of two days telling me that I should just let the storm hit and help with the clean up effort afterward.

I told her that I might possibly have the power to stop it, and therefore I am responsible for doing whatever I could possibly do.

"Yeah," I said. "I haven't been sleeping much lately...something's been on my mind."

"When is the storm projected to hit?"

"This afternoon," I answered.

"What's the plan?"

I hadn't really thought of a plan, but there was no way I was going to tell Sheila as much.

"I figured I'll head out after lunch and make my way to the coast and wait for it to come."

"And then what?"

"Then, I fight it."

I tried to sound brave, but I knew and she knew that I didn't have a clue. And she knew that I certainly wasn't feeling brave about the whole thing.

Principal Lipscolm came out of the building just at the right time, as it seemed Sheila and I had run out of awkward things to say to each other.

He had a very serious look on his face. I'd seen this a few weeks ago, but this time it seemed even more dire, as if that was even possible.

Grabbing the top of my arm in his hand, he dragged me to his office and sat me down in the chair opposite his desk.

"Is there any way — "

"I'm on it," I said putting a hand up. "I've got this under control."

I'm not sure who my hubris surprised more, me or him. But there it was, all out on the table. I was going to have to pull something off. And it was going to have to be something miraculous.

* * *

Have you ever stood on the beach and watched the waves of the oceans crashing against each other from a distance? The white foam that forms is beautiful and keeps us there, transfixed at its majesty.

But what happens when the force that results in that wondrous white foam reaches land?

I didn't want to find out, but I knew I was going to.

The storm was coming, like a wall. A wall full of malice and destruction.

I looked down the left side of the beach — empty.

And then the right side of the beach — empty as well.

This was good.

The only thing worse than trying to save the world, is trying to save the world with someone, or a lot of someones watching. My palms get all sweaty and my mouth goes dry. Even my thoughts stop flowing.

So, I was pretty relieved not to have an audience.

I looked up into the sky and noticed the seagulls were all flying around haphazardly, like they didn't know in which direction to go. Eventually, they began flying toward me, which was my cue to get my game face on!

And sure enough, just as fast as those birds began heading toward me, so did the ocean. The waves were so high. They seemed almost as high as the buildings I was admiring just a few days earlier.

They were coming fast and they were coming hard and I had no idea what to do. I had two days, three if you count the first day I heard about the storm, and yet I'd come up with nothing.

In a moment of desperation, I took a deep breath, closed my eyes and discovered a new power.

As I stretched my arms out wide and began to rise, it felt as if a force field of sorts, a giant barrier between the storm and the city was emanating from me. And as the waves were just about upon me, ready to crash into the wall I'd created, I took a brief moment to wonder just what side of the barrier I was on.

Obviously, I'd hoped that I was on the city side and not the water side, but that was not the case.

The water hit me with such force that all of the air in my body shot out of it. Cold water rushed against me and my head instantly began to ache, like when I eat ice cream too fast, but without the joy of the ice cream. And it didn't let up after thirty seconds like a normal brain freeze would have.

I fought the urge to curl up like a ball for warmth. I was afraid of what might happen if I broke my concentration and pulled my arms in. I thought that maybe the wall I'd created would disappear and render this entire exercise useless.

So there I hung, suspended in mid-air, arms out, cold water hitting me like a sledge hammer and my face feeling like it was being pelted by tiny needles from the driving rain.

I took a glance behind me and noticed that people were starting to gather. People who'd been previously hiding for cover, had now come out from their spots and were taking the opportunity to marvel at the spectacle that was me.

As if that wasn't bad enough, the cell phones started coming out. No doubt, I'd be an internet sensation by the end of tomorrow.

Great, I thought to myself. That's just what I need...more attention.

It's hard to live in a day and age where everyone is trying to get noticed and everyone wants someone else's attention. And then there's me. I just want to be left alone.

But because I have this burdensome gift of super powers, I have to constantly put myself in a position to be admired and photographed and the whole nine. Honestly, at that moment, I just wanted to drop down to the ground and let the storm swallow them all up.

But that would've been wrong. Really wrong.

So, I kept on going with my 'force', if that's even what it's called.

At one point, it seemed like things were going to let up and I was starting to feel slightly relieved. This was short lived, however. The ocean drew back and when it charged again, it came at me with massive tornado like spouts.

They popped up all over the place.

And as if it wasn't bad enough having water hurled at me through incredibly fast wind vortexes, they had managed to pick up sea debris.

Yeah, that's right...junk from the water.

Everything you could think of.

Live fish, dead fish, boots, tires, buoys, and even a few license plates.

I was somehow able to dodge most of these items. I'm not sure how badly they would've hurt me, to be honest with you. But I was glad not to find out. There was one fish however, that I was unable to avoid. It was a big boy fish, black and shiny, and fully alive...until it hit me.

I didn't actually see it die. And I'd like to think that maybe it lived. But it hit me in the face so hard and dropped like a boulder, straight down to the beach below me that there's no way it could've survived. The water was rushing in and out so fast that by the time I was able to look down toward the ground, the fish was gone...and my face was throbbing.

Eventually the storm died down. I'd outlasted it, and though I was still alive, it hadn't come without a cost.

I was exhausted and my body was freezing and sore. My extremities were throbbing and the water I must've swallowed while suspended in mid air came out in one tremendous wretch.

When I looked up, Sheila was standing over me.

"When did you get here?" I panted.

"A few minutes ago," she said.

I looked around at the people gathered. There must've been hundreds, possibly thousands, most of whom were standing in front of me with their cell phones up, pushing buttons on their touch screens that I could only imagine were sending my image to who knows where.

"How did you know where I was?"

"I saw it on TV," Sheila said. "You're all over the news. Everybody knows everything about what you did. You're a famous super hero, JW!"

"Great," I said. "Here we go again."

A SHORT STORY FOR KIDS AGES 9-12

GRADE SCHOOL 3
SUPER HERO
JUST ANOTHER DAY

JUSTIN JOHNSON

GRADE SCHOOL SUPER HERO 3
JUST ANOTHER DAY

Hey there, JW here!

By now, no doubt, you've heard of me and my super powers.

It's been about a year since I saved the city from complete death and destruction from the massive 'Storm of the Century'.

Do you remember how I told you the last time that fame was fleeting; that it wouldn't last more than a few weeks before it all went away?

Well, I need to take a second to address that. When I said that, I hadn't taken into account the power of the internet and cell phone cameras.

You see, when I saved the world from the asteroid, nobody had their cell phones out while I was actually battling the asteroid. Sure, they were out afterward and during interviews and parades in the week that followed. And my meeting with the President was on all of the national news channels. My parents even received digital copies of the press conference from the White House...but even they don't much talk about it or bring it up anymore.

Now, this last adventure I had, the one where I saved the city from the storm, there were cameras everywhere. And they recorded the whole event in its entirety. And then they posted everything on various websites and video sites and everything else.

Long story short, it went viral. If you don't know what viral is, that means that the word and video spread very quickly and a lot of people found out about what I'd done in a short period of time.

So, I would like to make an amendment to my previous statement on the short lived nature of fame. Fame does not typically last long, however, when everyone in the city has their cell phones pointed at you when you're suspended fifty feet in the air, projecting a force field that is stopping millions of gallons of ocean water from decimating the city you live in and all of its inhabitants, then fame can last a little longer.

Sheila and I couldn't walk anywhere without being stopped. I was usually asked to sign autographs and jump really high, like they'd all heard I could do. Often, I would sign whatever piece of paper they shoved in my face, so long as they had a pen. But I refuse to jump on command. After all, I'm not a dog.

* * *

I was hopeful that a summer off and away from school would curb things a little. Sheila and I hung out quite a bit during the summer, but it was always at her house or mine. We'd stopped going to the park or the mall, or even just walking down the street.

And finally, it was time for school to begin again.

My hopes that people would forget over the summer were dashed before I even walked up the front steps. There were mobs of kids standing around, phones pulled out and posters made. They were almost blocking the entire staircase, making it difficult for Sheila and I to make our way up to the door.

When I got to my first class of the day, Mrs. Winslow had her projector board fired up and was running an internet news site from her computer. I recognized it as the local news channel my parents watched every night. But the normal news people were not there. There were two younger women telling us the things the usual team would, no doubt, be telling us later on in the day.

I noticed Mrs. Winslow looked very concerned.

Her face never moved from the screen and she had her hand placed in front of her half opened mouth. This is very strange for any teacher to do on any day of school, but on the first day of school it's a definite signal that something's about to go terribly wrong.

Before I could even begin to focus on the newscast, I felt a lead ball drop in my stomach. Overwhelming nausea and dizziness took over my senses.

And then I heard the words: Possible Earthquake.

That's when I passed out.

* * *

When I came to, I was in the nurse's office. The nurse was leaning over me with a small plastic cup filled with something that looked like pee.

"Have some apple juice honey," she said sweetly. "It'll help you get back on your feet. We have some cookies too, if you'd like."

I smiled and she brought me a package of chocolate cookies with white frosting in the middle.

"How are you feeling?" she asked. "You had quite the nasty fall in the classroom."

As soon as she mentioned the fall, I felt a spot on the right side of my head begin to throb and I noticed my hand was holding something cold.

I gave her a puzzled look and she continued.

"Your teacher says you fell down and hit your head on the marker tray in front of the board. You were lucky it didn't cut your head right open."

I nodded. "How long have I been down here?"

"Oh, not too terribly long. An hour, maybe less."

"Can you tell me about the earthquake?"

"Oh, JW...you shouldn't be worrying your head about an earthquake right now. You need to put your energy into getting that noggin better and getting some juice into your system to help keep you upright."

I handed her the juice and cookies and stood up.

She put her hand out and warned, "I wouldn't do that if I were you, honey."

It took me a second to realize what she meant, the rush of blood from my brain almost made me lose consciousness again, but I managed to maintain my balance.

Little flickering dots were floating all around my field of vision and my foot was heavy as I took my first step. Gradually they became easier.

The only thought going through my mind was that the city was in trouble yet again, and it was up to me to save it!

* * *

I probably shouldn't be telling you this, but I left school in a rush. I skipped class and didn't sign out through the main office.

If I was going to be able to do anything I needed to do to keep the city and its people safe from harm, I was going to have to be able to move without being noticed. I couldn't run the risk of not getting where I needed to because of a giant swarm of people wanting to get my autograph or take a selfie with me.

When I got to my house, I turned on the TV in the kitchen. As usual, the local news was tuned in and all I had to do was sit at the kitchen table.

My parents were still at work, as most normal folks would be at this hour of the day. The house seemed a little creepy without them, to be perfectly honest with you.

I sat down in my father's chair, just to see how it felt to be him. His view of the TV was kind of awkward. From this position, he would have to turn his body and his head to his left, which looked like second nature to him, but for me seemed very uncomfortable.

I decided that it would be better for me to stand in my normal spot, over by the counter.

One of the ladies on the TV was talking about something called a fault. She said that this was basically a giant crack in the earth and sometimes the crack moved or shifted, causing an earthquake. She seemed to think, along with her co-anchor and someone called a seismologist, who was an expert on earthquakes, that the fault located just below our city was due to have one of those shifts and the results would be catastrophic, of course.

I kept my eyes glued to the television, hoping to get any kind of clue that might help me figure out what I had to do to stop this thing from happening. It took a few minutes, but then the seismologist said the words I needed to hear.

"If I had to guess, based on the data we've collected and things like this we've seen in the past, I would say that this is likely to hit this afternoon."

This afternoon! How could they have missed this? How is it they were just starting to let people know that they would do well to evacuate the city and take all of their important possessions with them?

Ok. I looked at the clock. It was just after 10 AM. I could definitely be in position to stop this thing. I just had to know where to go.

The man on the TV said that epicenter of this particular fault was somewhere between 8th and 30th street in the business district.

Oh great, I thought to myself. Nothing like having to try to cover 22 blocks in the busiest section of the city when you're already kind of famous.

It was becoming clear to me that this was going to be my most challenging task yet.

It was a relatively warm day, just the beginning of fall. The leaves were starting to change on the trees and it was one of those days where everyone wanted to be out and about, walking their dogs or shopping for fresh foods at the outside markets.

I live in a pretty big city and these markets are spread out for quite a distance, up and down the sidewalks for blocks at a time.

My chances of getting through this whole thing unrecognized seemed unlikely.

I walked with my head down to 8th street. I figured I would start there and look for any sign of activity that might be caused by two giant rocks shifting beneath the pavement.

It became apparent after a while that nobody had really heard about the earthquake; nobody down here anyway.

Everyone seemed to be acting like it was just another day, which made sense. If they were just out walking their dogs and enjoying the nice fall day...they wouldn't have heard the news yet.

And hopefully by the time this thing was supposed to rear its ugly head, I could have stopped it and made the whole thing non-existent.

I was just getting on to 21st street when I noticed something in the middle of the road. And let me tell you, this thing was nothing noticeable. I really had to look to see it, but it was there and, to me anyway, it was a clear indication of the center of the fault.

The tiniest of cracks in the pavement had started to form. It was fresh. I could tell because the little pieces of asphalt were still sitting on the edge of either side of he crack.

I stood on the sidewalk, waiting for the cars to clear out.

Just as I was getting ready to step foot into the road, I heard a shout.

"Hey, isn't that the super hero kid?"

And that was all it took.

There were people everywhere.

Cell phones at the ready.

Purses and pockets were being checked for spare pieces of paper and pens.

Instinctively, I moved out to the road, more to get away from the crowd that was in the process of closing in on me than to check what I'd originally come down here for.

And then I felt it. It wasn't big, and I wasn't even sure anyone else had felt it.

It started right under my sneaker, a vibration.

It wasn't obvious, almost like the humming of a refrigerator that's been running for a while. You know it's there, but you don't think much of it.

Except this was right below my foot and there was no way I couldn't think much of it, given what I'd heard earlier.

My muscles tightened and jerked, almost involuntarily, as the slow steady hum of seismic waves resonated inside of my body. They ran right up through my feet and then my legs began wobbling like a couple of jelly filled molds.

I looked up at the approaching mob and saw in their faces that this had not gripped them. They pressed forward woefully unaware that anything was even happening.

This was the moment. I could feel it. I knew I had to something, but I had no idea what that something was going to be.

Until I did it.

I just jumped down on the ground, spread out like an asterisk on the pavement, my hands and legs on either side of the fault crack, my body directly on top of it running parallel.

I guess in that moment, if you were there and you knew what was going on, you might describe me as a human band aid, or more specifically a butterfly bandage. Those are the ones that have little arms and legs coming off of them. They're designed to hold things intact, keep the two sides of the cut together. That's what I looked like, trying to hold the middle of the road together.

I'd find out later, that I looked nothing like what I thought, but we'll save that for later.

Car horns were starting to beep and angry drivers were shouting out of their windows. They were yelling things like, "Get outta the way kid!" and "What are you thinking, we've got places to go!" and "You're going to get yourself killed out here in the middle of the road!"

I kept my head down, my face was now resting on the warm fall pavement and then the first surge hit. It went through my body like a jolt of electricity. It was a small one, but there was still a level of discomfort.

Part of me was hoping that any future jolts would be less significant, because this last one was kind of painful, plus I almost peed my pants.

I brought my head up momentarily, just to check out the situation. It seemed like no one else had felt what I had.

I put my head back down and settled in for some more.

And then surge two came.

* * *

Now, it really kind of bothers me to tell you this, but it would be wrong for me not to. There were a few moments, during the course of saving the city from the earthquake, that I felt like giving up. I felt like standing up and letting the whole thing just take right over and shake the very guts out of everything around us.

To the average onlooker...actually, to all of the onlookers, I just looked like some kid lying down in the middle of the street doing some weird looking dance on the cement.

They had no idea what I was going through, the pain my body was experiencing. And, honestly, I don't mind taking on this level of burden — when it's appreciated.

But this crowd had their phones out, recording, while I slid from side to side, my face rubbing hard against the road, giving my cheeks and nose blisters that would take months to heal.

They started laughing as my body was thrust up and down and back and forth, slamming against the crack that had formed as a result of the fault. Each time I moved, it was because of a seismic wave grabbing hold of my insides and doing whatever it wanted. It was painful and I winced more than a few times, trying to keep from crying.

I started to wonder how long this thing was going to go on. How much longer could it possible keep shaking me, rocking me to my core, while the giant plates of rock shifted far below the ground, rubbing harshly against each other, creating havoc of the worst kind?

I felt a jolt.

It was by far the worst pain I'd felt yet. It shot right through my stomach and traveled through my intestines, shaking free some stuff that would have been better left stuck in place. Once it was through my digestive system, the reverberations reached the base of my spine and rattled their way up my back. It gave me the appearance of doing the worm dance, until it reached the top of my spine and entered my skull, quickly snapping my head back down to the pavement.

The throbbing in my nose was fast and steady. I could almost feel my heart beating in my face as drops of blood fell on the pavement just below my eyes.

After that, all went quiet and still for a few moments.

I pushed myself half up, propping on my left arm and wiping the blood from my face with my right hand. I was pleasantly surprised to feel that I wasn't bleeding as badly as I'd thought.

My little pocket of joy was short lived, however. When I looked up and saw that everyone on the street had either a cell phone, a camera, or a strange and uncomfortable smile on their face. They were the types of smiles that wanted to turn into outright laughter, but since the subject of their amusement was on the ground in front of them, and they knew it would be rude to really let loose, they held them in, surely waiting to get home and put on the video for a friend. This way they could get a bowl of popcorn and hit the replay button as much as they wanted, while they laughed haughtily into the night.

I took a deep breath and let out a giant sigh just as I felt something twitching beneath my toes. It was time to put my head down and go to work again.

The vibration started slowly, moving up through my toes and into the middle of my foot.   It didn't feel so bad at first, and actually kind of tickled.

By the time it had moved up to my knees, the small joy that the tickles had brought me were over.   The pain was so excruciating, my knees felt like the bones were being crushed into powder by Thor's giant hammer.

I tried hard not to cry, knowing that everyone was watching. No doubt, some of them would be zooming right in on my face.   Big tears and bloodshot eyes would certainly bring joy and laughter to a number of viewers around the world.

I couldn't help it.   My tears came...and came...and came.

They were followed, as tears usually are, by massive amounts of snot and mucous.   I could feel my face go flush, red as could be, before the geyser that is my nose opened up all over the pavement.

The vibrations had made their way up to my chest while all of this was happening.   I could feel my heart fighting hard inside my rib cage to keep the shock at bay.

I didn't mean to scream, but I couldn't help it. The crushing force of seismic waves just forced it out of me. I'd like to think it sounded at least a little manly. But truth be told, the laughter I heard from the onlookers, let me know I had sounded like a girl. And probably a super wimpy girl at that.

That's a funny thing about being a super hero. You're expected to sound a certain way — tough and rugged — but honestly, I just can't pull that off.

Finally, the force had made its way up to my head. It was weird. It felt like a giant sumo wrestler had decided to use my forehead for a chair, which seemed strange, because there was nothing on top of me.

I closed my eyes and took a slow, deep breath, trying to go to my happy place. I feared that if I wasn't able to block out how much it hurt, that I'd end up letting go and the whole city would fall to its knees.

I held on as tightly as I could, gritting my teeth and dealing with the pain the best I knew how.

"You look ridiculous," said a voice from behind me.

I knew this voice, knew it well.

"Sheila?!" I grunted through my gnashed teeth. "What does it look like I'm doing? I'm saving the city, again."

"How's it going?" she asked.

Bringing my head up, I looked around to see the people who'd gathered. I noticed everyone was still standing with their phones out. Some of them were laughing, others were smirking, trying to hold it in, and yet others were taking pity on me, looking at me as though I had a serious problem, which was most certainly, not funny.

"I think I'm almost done," I answered. At least, I hoped I was.

* * *

In the end, I laid there, sprawled out on the concrete for a further forty-five minutes. I guess I'd refused to let go for two reasons.

One, of course, was the fear of what might happen if I were to let my guard down for even a second. That last rush of seismic friction was pretty intense, and the thought of what could've been had I not been there had made a pretty big impact on my brain.

The other reason is one I feel quite guilty about actually talking about. But I've been completely honest so far, so why stop now, right? The truth is that I stayed there on the street, with my head down, for so long because I knew that once I got up, I'd have to face the music. Or, in this case, the fact that I was now a celebrity again. Famous — or rather, infamous — for having done a silly dance in the middle of mid-town traffic through lunch hour. Guilty for having held up hundreds and thousands of people from getting where they wanted to go, keeping them from a nice meal with their sweetheart, or their only chance during the day to go shopping.

It was all my fault.

And soon the world would know about it again.

I'd be at home, watching myself on the evening news, or worse yet - Youtube. People forget about the evening news. It's gone in a matter of days. But on the internet, videos and pictures live on forever. People remember them and comment about them and share them with their friends. And just when you think people have started to forget, someone whips out their phone and holds a video of you, looking ridiculous while trying to save the world, and asks, "Dude, is that you?"

And all you can do is shrug.

Because in the life of a superhero, the unfortunate thing is, that it was just another day.

TURN THE PAGE FOR A

SPECIAL

SNEAK PEEK

OF

WILD JUNGLE

1

The plane began to shake. The pilot's voice had come over the speaker system an hour earlier, like the great and powerful Oz, and announced something called turbulence.

Jake Lennon hadn't been familiar with the term before that moment. But after fifteen minutes, that felt like three hours, of jostling around in his seat, closing his eyes tight and trying to think of anything else that might allow him to keep his dinner and warm apple juice from finding the back of the seat in front of him, he knew what it was. And he didn't like it.

He didn't like it almost as much as he didn't like the idea of being on this plane in the first place. The seats were cramped, even for a boy of ten, whose mother had even said herself that he'd just gone through a major growth spurt. And yet she'd subjected him to this tiny little seat on this sardine box in the sky anyway. The plane was mere commuter jet, at least that's what he'd heard his mother say. There were maybe fifty seats, and half of them weren't even full.

The food was horrible, and he feared that if they hit another bout of 'the turbulence', that he would have to taste it again. Only this time, it would be on the way up and out, which he knew from experience tasted much worse.

"Please turn off all cell phones and other communication devices," the voice of Oz had said.

Jake had had his headphones on at the time. He hadn't heard the announcement, but his father thought that he was just being difficult and took his phone away. His father stuffed it into his pocket and handed Jake an issue of a magazine he'd gotten from the back of the seat in front of him, which Jake could tell would be useless and boring.

He could hardly blame his father for thinking that he was being difficult. He'd been difficult all morning, truth be told. When they'd told him about the family vacation to South America three weeks earlier, he'd been less than enthusiastic.

The thought of family vacations, or anything that took him out of his bedroom for more than an hour, made Jake a little grumpy. There was nothing he'd rather do than play video games with his friends. And video games weren't going to be available to him when they arrived at their destination. According to his parents, this was going to be a real 'wilderness' experience.

"That sounds like it's going to be a lot of fun," Jake had said. These had been the words his parents had been hoping to hear, but the tone was not. Rather than excitement, Jake had decided to fill this sentence with snark and sarcasm. His parents had secretly debated whether they should let Jake just stay with his Uncle Tommy for the week. But eventually, they decided that it would be good for him to get out and experience something real. And it would be a good bonding experience for the family.

So far, thanks to Jake's father taking his phone away, and all of the turbulence, the vacation was off to a very bumpy start.

And now that the plane was shaking again, Jake was just trying to do whatever he could to ensure that he made it to the ground without anything else going wrong.

"Are you okay?" his father asked. "You don't look so good. Do you feel like you're going to be sick?"

He glared at his father. "Of course I feel sick, the plane's moving up and down like a roller coaster."

"Here," his mother said. She was reaching out her hand, which was holding a small plastic cup full of an amber colored liquid. "It's Ginger Ale. It'll help."

Jake shook his head 'no' and pushed the cup back toward his mother. A large jolt sent the cup flying from his mother's hands and onto his father's lap. Much to Jake's surprise, his father didn't say a word. He gritted his teeth and blew a tremendous amount of air through his nose.

It sounded like he might have been getting ready to give Jake a stern talking to, when there was a crash. It was loud and sudden. The plane jerked to the right, forcing Jake to look out the window.

He had to rub his eyes and do a double take before he could be sure about the source of the crash. But after a few moments he realized that the wing on his side of the plane had fallen off.

2

Jake stared in disbelief at what was left of the plane's right wing, a mess of mangled and curled up metal and wires. He brought his attention back inside the plane. His father was still looking upset about the ginger ale spill and his mother was apologizing, saying it was all her fault.

The other passengers looked to be coping with the turbulence. They had their hands on the arm rests, and while some of them had white knuckles from holding on tightly, most of them seemed fine.

How could they just sit here and act like nothing had happened? Had they not heard the crash? Had they not looked out the window to see for themselves that the wing had broken free and fallen off?

There was another crash and Jake could see sparks and flames outside the left side of the plane. He had a sinking feeling inside that the other wing had just been ripped off by something outside, probably a lightning bolt.

He reached down and unfastened his seat belt.

"Buckle yourself back up," his father said, eyeing him.

"But there's…" Jake stood up to survey the rest of the plane, letting his words trail off. Nobody. Not a single person doing anything that would indicate that the plane was on the verge of going down.

"Honey," his mother chimed in, hoping that he would just sit down and save himself some trouble. "Why don't you do what your father says and sit down?"

Jake turned toward the back of the plane. He could feel his father's hand on his arm, pulling him back down into his seat.

And then he saw her. She was sitting near the back of the plane on the left. Her blond haired pig tails and pink Dora bag, gave the Jake the impression that she couldn't have been any older than four or five. She was in a panic. A woman next to her was trying to calm her down, shoving books and small packages of fruit snacks in front of her face.

Jake's father pulled him back into his seat before he could see whether the woman's attempts at distracting the child were successful. The child's continued cries were a strong indicator that the her efforts had failed.

"What's going on with you?" Jake's father asked.

"There's something happening —"

His answer was cut short by another cry of sorts. This time, it was more of a scream, coming from the front of the plane, a few seats ahead of Jake.

"What's gotten into him?" A man asked. His voice had an edge to it, but it was more from concern than anger.

"I don't know," A woman answered. "He was fine just a moment ago."

The boy continued to scream, gaining the attention of the flight attendant. A portly man in a blue vest shuffled up the aisle toward the family, his hips rubbing the edges of the seats as he made his way. He had a stern look on his face, which was becoming redder with every step he took. By the time he reached the family, he was breathing heavily and had to take a moment to compose himself before speaking.

"Son," he said, addressing the boy and not his parents. "Excuse me." He waited and watched as the boy continued his fit. "Young man!" he finally boomed.

The boy continued to scream and shout in hysterics. And now his father joined him, standing up and directing every ounce of his ire toward the attendant, whose eyes had the appearance of tea saucers.

"You will not speak to my son like that! If you have any problem with anyone in my family, you speak with me!"

The attendant's mouth dropped open and hung numbly from the his face. He shook his head back and forth, looking for help, as his jowls swayed from side to side. Another flight attendant came walking toward the situation from the front of the plane.

"What seems to be the problem?" She asked. She was thin with brown hair that hung in a tight braid down the middle of her back. She wore the same airline issued uniform as the man, but hers fit better.

The first attendant tried to update her on the situation, but his mouth still wasn't working. "Ub...a...eh...this...er..."

She put a finger up in the air and turned to the angry passenger.

"Sir, could you please help me understand what's going on here?"

Before he could get out a response, Jake felt the plane begin its descent.

3

The descent was swift. Not at all like landing, but more like the plane was going to crash. Heading toward the ground that fast could yield only one result.

Jake continued to look around, wondering why only he and the two kids, whose cries of fear were deafening, were noticing that the plane was going down.

Jake turned to the back of the plane and spotted the little girl with the Dora backpack. She'd curled up like a ball, her head tucked deep in her bag, her feet and legs closing her off from the rest of the world.

And then there was the situation with the flight attendants up front.

Oddly, as everybody craned their necks to get a good view of the show, nobody seemed to notice that the plane was headed toward earth at a rapid rate. They continued to eat their airline chicken and drink their warm soda, but were generally unconcerned.

Jake looked at his own parents, who were looking at him.

"Are you doing better now?" his father asked. He had a grin on his face and nodded in the direction of the boy in front of them. "You know, Jake, sometimes I don't give you enough credit. I see boys like that, who have no idea how to behave in public, and I can't help but think...you're a pretty great kid." He sat back in his seat, puffing his chest out with pride, a satisfied look on his face.

"Dad," Jake said, "don't you know why they're acting like that?"

"Nope. And I don't care." He gave Jake a wink.

"The plane's going down, dad." Jake turned to his mother. "Don't you feel that mom?"

"Now that's ridiculous!" His father said quietly, so as not to draw any attention.

Jake looked out the window again and there was a flash of light. It was a wide band of white light that seemed to envelope every side of the plane, like it was flying through a ring of fire.

It lasted little more than a second, and again, Jake could tell the boy and little girl had seen it, and the adults had not.

When the light had subsided, and Jake was no longer seeing floating spots, he looked out the window. Horror filled his heart as his lungs evacuated themselves of any air.

The last thing Jake Lennon saw was the tops of the trees, just before the plane hit them, and his mother looking at him through concerned eyes. He was conscious when she asked, "Jake? Are you alright?"

And then he wasn't.

DON'T FORGET TO
GET YOUR FREE BOOK!

For your free copy of the #1 Best Seller Farty Marty,
go to <u>www.justinjohnsonauthor.com</u>

ABOUT THE AUTHOR

Justin Johnson is a school teacher who loves writing stories for the kids he teaches.
He lives in Hastings, NY with his family.

Also by Justin Johnson

Complete Series Books
The Complete Coby Collins
Zack and Zebo
Scab and Beads

Short Story Collections
Farty Marty and Other Stories
Do Not Feed the Zombies and Other Stories
Grade School Super Hero: The Complete Trilogy

Individual Short Stories (eBook Only)
Farty Marty
Skeeter Skunk and the Glandular Funk
Flick
Grade School Super Hero
Grade School Super Hero 2: Here We Go Again
Grade School Super Hero 3: Just Another Day
Do Not Feed the Zombies
The Kick
Sarah and the Search for the Pot of Gold
The Dance Recital
A Kid in King William's Court

Novellas
The Card

42118188R00068

Made in the USA
San Bernardino, CA
27 November 2016